NEVER ENDING NIGHT MARE

© Copyright 2004 Michelle Michini.
All rights reserved. No part of this publication may be reproduced, stored in a retrieval system, or transmitted, in any form or by any means, electronic, mechanical, photocopying, recording, or otherwise, without the written prior permission of the author.

Note for Librarians: a cataloguing record for this book that includes Dewey Decimal Classification and US Library of Congress numbers is available from the Library and Archives of Canada. The complete cataloguing record can be obtained from their online database at:
www.collectionscanada.ca/amicus/index-e.html
ISBN 1-4120-4600-9

TRAFFORD

Offices in Canada, USA, Ireland, UK and Spain
This book was published on-demand in cooperation with Trafford Publishing. On-demand publishing is a unique process and service of making a book available for retail sale to the public taking advantage of on-demand manufacturing and Internet marketing. On-demand publishing includes promotions, retail sales, manufacturing, order fulfilment, accounting and collecting royalties on behalf of the author.

Book sales for North America and international:
Trafford Publishing, 6E–2333 Government St.,
Victoria, BC v8t 4p4 CANADA
phone 250 383 6864 (toll-free 1 888 232 4444)
fax 250 383 6804; email to orders@trafford.com

Book sales in Europe:
Trafford Publishing (uk) Ltd., Enterprise House, Wistaston Road Business Centre,
Wistaston Road, Crewe, Cheshire cw2 7rp UNITED KINGDOM
phone 01270 251 396 (local rate 0845 230 9601)
facsimile 01270 254 983; orders.uk@trafford.com

Order online at:
www.trafford.com/robots/04-2408.html

10 9 8 7 6 5 4 3 2 1

1

It was a cold day on January 13th, 1968. Leona was rushed to General Hospital in downtown Kansas City. Joe her husband of two years was with her. The nurses ignored Leona's screams of anguish as her seventh child was about to be born. Back in those days, Blacks were not treated very well. At three a.m. Leona's daughter Michelle was born. It was not exactly a happy event, after all, Leona did not care for her previous children and there was a national warrant out for her arrest. It did not take long for Leona and Joe to escape to California in search of a better life and to avoid arrest. Life was not easy for them for they both were street criminals always committing petty crimes.

Leona's life was not easy, mainly for the fact that Joe was a tyrant, drug and alcohol user that constantly dealt with her using an iron fist. One day Leone and Joe were cooking dinner together when they started fighting and arguing. Leona wanted to use drugs and Joe wanted her to finish dinner. Joe picked up a knife and held it to her throat, Leona struggled to get away but couldn't. Neighbors could hear their fighting and called the police. When the police arrived, they discovered Leona and Joe were wanted for bank robbery and they were arrested on the spot. The poor little baby Michelle was taken into custody by the California Child Protection unit where her fate was debated. After many court dates, Joseph was sentenced to 25 years in a state prison in Missouri and Leona was sentenced to ten. Daisy, Joseph's mother was very saddened by the fact that her only living son was locked away and only a little concerned that her granddaughter, Michelle was in the hands of California Child Protection. A social worker came to see Leona at the Prison where she was at to discuss the fate off her child. Ms. Tibbs suggested she put the little girl up for adoption since she never took care of any of her children and she was a drug addict and a criminal. Leona finally agreed that the best interest for her child was to be adopted. Ms. Tibbs informed her that there were people in California interested in adopting Michelle. At the suggestion of Ms. Tibbs, Leona signed the adoption papers and gave up all maternal rights and responsibilities. Now, Ms. Tibbs had to get Joe's signature since he was the legal father. Joe was a hardened criminal always in and out of jail, an alcoholic, drug user, thief and could not take care of a newborn baby. Ms. Tibbs tried for two months to persuade him to give up his parental rights and allow Michelle to be adopted by a more suitable couple. The couple in California who wanted to adopt Michelle were wealthy, prosperous people. The husband was a movie producer and his wife was an attorney in the entertainment industry. The couple did all they could to adopt Michelle, but failed because looser Joe did not want to give up his parental rights. Leona and Joe fought constantly via the court system while they were both incarcerated about the fate of Michelle. Leona's family had long ago washed their hands of her and offered no help. Joe's family had always forgiven him for his behavior and put up with whatever he dished out. They constantly visited him in prison, sent him money, put up property to set bail. Time and time again Joe's family especially his mother Daisy, rewarded his vicious, violent behavior. As far as Michelle goes, none of Joe's family members offered to take Michelle in, who knows the reason. Mama Daisy claimed she was too ill with a lung disease to help, but she said she knew one of her friends who was childless that would be interested in adopting Michelle. Mama Daisy contacted her friend Katherine and told her about her son's being in prison and that he refused to let anyone adopt the child for fear that he may never see the child again. Katherine and her husband who were 65 years at the time agreed to take Michelle. Joe and his Mama Daisy made the couple agree to taking Michelle and raising her but allowing only Joe and his family to have unlimited contact with her. This was the biggest mistake Katherine and her husband Henry ever made with Michelle. The one decision to allow this madman Joe into little Michelle's life later turned out to be the one thing that ruined this innocent little girls life for along time. Michelle arrived at Katherine and Henry's home in June1968. Michelle had been staying in foster care out in California where Joe and Leona were first arrested. Katherine and Henry were an older couple in their late sixties who were successful. Henry was a contractor and a minister, who built his own home and his own church on property that he owned out in the country in Kansas. Henry was also a farmer, who had cattle, hogs, chickens and grew his own peaches and had huge vegetable gardens. Henry's wife Katherine, was a retired nurse who stayed at home to take care of Michelle. Katherine and Henry loved Michelle with all of their heart and held nothing from her. Katherine was so happy to get Michelle. She went out of her way spoiling her with fancy clothes, dolls and fixed up her a special nursery with everything in it. Michelle had a stable loving home living with Katherine and Henry. Every Sunday, Michelle went to Henry's church and the congregation would fuss over little Michelle. The congregation for a long time would give extra money in the collection plates for Michelle's well being. Henry's niece and nephew that lived next door, Marge and HenryRobert, would also help Katherine with Michelle. Often Marge who was young and had children of her own, would baby-sit Michelle while Katherine would work part-time. The property that Katherine and Henry lived on had 50 acres so there was plenty of room for Michelle to play on when she started walking. Due to the fact that Katherine and Henry agreed to let Joe's family have unlimited contact with Michelle, Mama Daisy and her daughters were constantly taking Michelle once a month to Moberly Missouri State Prison to visit Joe. This went on since Michelle was six months old. The agreement was that Leona, the natural mother of Michelle, was never to visit or have any contact with Michelle. This decision outraged Leona and her family. Leona with the help of the police officer who later became her husband, helped her get an early prison release after three years. It was believed that Joe had forced Leona to rob a bank with him. Many people believed it, so they released her from prison early, while Joe served his full sentence of 15 years. One day Leona decided to trespass onto Katherine's property to steal Michelle. Leona rang the doorbell and Katherine answered. Leona forced her way into the home and stole Michelle. Katherine was frantic and called the police who eventually returned Michelle. This action led Katherine and Henry to change Michelle's last name to Smith. It was not a fully legal procedure since Joe refused to sign adoption papers for Michelle to be adopted by them. They never went to court to have the last name legally changed and it did not change the birth certificate. Michelle was sheltered, loved and protected by Katherine and Henry for five years until Henry developed kidney disease and passed away in April 1973. Michelle knew something was not right with Henry when he started vomiting after meals. Soon trips to Providence Hospital were frequent to visit Henry. While Katherine visited Henry in the hospital, Michelle was kept company in the hospital area reception room by her cousins, Tracy and Den. Michelle got comfort through gazing at the Virgin Mary statue that was in the hallway that led to her daddy's room. The visits were pleasant waiting with Tracy and Den who always bought green onion potato chips from the gift shop to munch on. The day finally came when Henry said good night for the last time. It was a rainy morning in April in 1973 when HenryRobert, Katherine's nephew by marriage drove Katherine to Providence Hospital for the last time. Michelle was allowed to say good bye to Henry and his last words were "take care of your mommy and be a good girl". Being only five years old, Michelle new her daddy would never come home. After HenryRobert drove Katherine home, Michelle remembers Katherine breaking down in HenryRobert's arms "be strong Ainey", HenryRobert said," everything will be alright". There must have been five hundred people at the funeral of Henry. It was a sunny pleasant day to be laid to rest. Katherine was dressed as a traditional widow, in a basic black dress, black pumps, black hat with a veil. Many tears were shed that day by many family and friends who loved Henry dearly. Michelle wept at her kindergarten class with her classmate Amy, who said her daddy died too. Life on the farm without Henry was lonely for Katherine and Michelle for awhile. But as they say, life goes on. A year later, Michelle started first grade. Michelle took the school bus to and from school, did homework, and played outside in her huge backyard. Holidays came and went. Christmases were always special to Michelle. Since Kansas got lots of snow back in the 70's, Michelle had fairytale Christmases. The house she lived in was out in the country, surrounded by woods. It was a medium sized red brick home with evergreen trees surrounding it. Thanksgiving and Christmas was always special for Michelle. The snow covering the woods made it even dreamier. For years, even when Henry was alive,

Thanksgiving and Christmas was always lively and exciting. Katherine's niece Geraldine with her husband Judge Brooks, would always come over with lots of great gifts for Katherine and Michelle. Their daughter, Casey was around Michelle's age, so they always played together. Ever since Michelle was six months old, Joseph was having his mother Daisy bring Michelle to visit him at the State Prison in Missouri. When Michelle was four years old, she remembered being forced to go with Daisy and her three daughters to visit Joseph at the prison. Michelle would scream and cry and refuse to go and Daisy would tell her that she was going to visit her dad who was in college. Michelle remembers that there were lots of policemen around, and there was a metal gate that she could not touch. Michelle could never bond with these people, and she did not feel any love for them especially Joseph. Michelle loved Katherine and Henry whom she knew as her mommy and daddy. For many years, Joseph would keep in contact with Michelle by calling and writing. Leona, Michelle's mother, was never allowed to visit her daughter, so she never knew that side of her family until she was thirteen years old. Katherine kept herself busy by babysitting children. She had mostly children of well to do families and a few from poorer families. Katherine was always more loving towards the children who were white or fairer skinned with a nice grade of hair. Being Black herself, but mixed with lots of American Indian, she naturally preferred children and people of lighter skin. Michelle was light brown when she was a child. Her hair had grown thick and to the middle of her back by the time she was eleven years old. Michelle developed early for her age. At eleven years old, she was 5'2, 110 pounds and wearing a 36 C bra, so she looked older than eleven years old. By 1979 Joseph was released from prison early. When he was released, he came around Michelle and was a very bad influence on her. The year was 1997 and it was a very bad year, the year that was the beginning of the end of Michelle's life. A never ending nightmare.

Joseph was a negative minded, violent tempered Black man when he was released from prison. He came around frequently to visit Michelle against Katherine's wishes. Katherine knew Joseph's reputation and never liked him. She felt very uncomfortable about him coming to her home. Behind Katherine's back, Joseph would tell Michelle about his Bonnie and Clyde lifestyle with Leona, glamorizing his criminal life. This information impressed Michelle who wanted to mimic this lifestyle. Joseph got himself an apartment in Kansas City Missouri and a job as a janitor. Joseph got himself a girlfriend named Linda who lived with him. She seemed okay. Linda was a registered nurse who worked at a nearby hospital. On weekends when Joseph would pick Michelle up, Joseph would let her sample his alcohol, soon Michelle wanted to drink on a regular basis. Joseph said to not tell Daisy his mother or anyone else. The shit really started to stink when in April 1979, Katherine and Michelle and Carlton, Katherine's nephew flew to Florida to attend Carlton's sisters debutante. On the way to Florida on the plane Michelle ordered a whiskey sour drink for the stewardess and was not asked for identification. She was only eleven years old. Katherine sat across from Michelle and gave her a look of disapproval but said nothing. When they arrived in Florida, Michelle met Carlton's baby sister and they got along well. The two younger girls were not allowed at the debutante and were left home alone while everyone attended the event. Michelle's first visit to Miami Beach was enjoyable. Lots of pictures were taken and lots of fun was had by all. When Katherine and Michelle returned home, Katherine decided to call Daisy and tell her that Michelle had ordered a whiskey sour on the plane. Daisy who portrays a highly religious woman, told Joseph and ordered him to spank Michelle. One day after school, Joseph shows up at Katherine's home with his girlfriend Linda. He orders Michelle into his car and tells her he wants to talk to her at his new apartment he has in Kansas. When they arrived at his apartment, Joseph drinks a pint of gin and tells Michelle that he did not appreciate her getting a drink on the plane.

He takes a belt and starts beating Michelle for at least thirty minutes. The child was terrified and confused for it was her own father that introduced alcohol to her in the first place. Bruises were left on Michelle's legs. When she returned home with Katherine, she cried in her mother's arms and asked her why she allowed Joseph to beat her? The next day when Michelle went to school, she told her teacher what happened and told her that she was afraid of her father. The principal called social services and Michelle was temporarily removed from Katherine's home. Two weeks later, Michelle went back home and was ordered to have family therapy with a lady named Betsy. After school one day Joseph comes back over to Katherine's and went into Michelle's room threatening to kill her if she told anyone about his ugly behavior. Michelle knew that something was not right about this individual and she wanted far away from Katherine's home, for it was not safe anymore.

3

Things really turned ugly when Katherine went to Washington D.C. for her annual family reunion. Michelle decided to stay with Joseph and Linda. This was the beginning of the end of a child ever having a chance of a normal life. Joseph and Linda took Michelle to her family therapy with Betsy. Betsy talked with Michelle with Joseph, then she talked to her by herself. Michelle had mentioned that she had overheard Joseph discussing committing a crime with Linda. Betsy betrayed her by revealing this to Joseph. After the session, Joseph badgered Michelle about what she told Betsy. He told Michelle that he was going to take her someplace since she thought it was a joke that he spent time in prison. Michelle was scared, not knowing what this crazy Black man was talking about. Joseph drove to the police station in Kansas City Kansas and made Michelle sit at a police officers desk. Michelle had done nothing wrong and did not deserve this treatment. Joseph talked to the police officer in private and Michelle later found out that Joseph told the police that she had pulled a knife on him. Michelle was led to a patty wagon and locked in. Michelle screamed and cried, for she did not know what was happening. She was taken to Kaw View jail for kids. Michelle was sitting in a cell with a toilet by herself. A staff member befriended her by talking to her and letting her smoke. Michelle had no idea where she was or why she was there. Michelle was pretty with a nice figure and looked older than she was, she remembers a guy who was at least sixteen having a crush on her, his name was T-bone. Two days later, Betsy, her family therapist got word of what Joseph had done. Betsy arrived at Kaw View and picked up Michelle and informed her that her own father had lied on her by telling the police that she had pulled a knife on him. Michelle remembers being numb, not having much feeling. When Katherine returned from her family reunion, she was not allowed to see Michelle until social services figured out what was going on. Michelle was put in a foster home. There were a lot of children there, two had lice eggs in their hair and it was Michelle who discovered it. Bonnie was her foster mother, she was a nice woman who was a beautician and she gave Michelle her first hair relaxer. Back then, Michelle's hair was long, thick and beautiful. Due to all of the confusion in Michelle's life she ran away from the foster home and got into the car of a strange man. The man was nice and never hurt Michelle, but Michelle told him she was 18. He tried to teach her to drive and he tried to pressure her into sleeping with him. He eventually dropped her off on Minnesota Avenue, where a man in a red Mustang picked her up. He asked her if she liked jazz and drove her to his home. It was a nice home out in west Kansas City Kansas. The man was Black and wore blue overalls. Michelle did not know what she was getting herself into. The man said his name was Tony. He forced himself on Michelle and took her virginity. He was a large man with a very large penis and this was very frightening for Michelle. The man threatened to hit her, called her a whore then drove her to a gas station at 3 in the morning and left her. A police officer pulled up and Michelle went to him and told him she was raped. The police went to the house of the man and wrote down some information then he took her to the emergency room. Her foster mother Bonnie came to get her and took her home. Stephanie, Bonnie's foster daughter who was 20 years old, did not like Michelle and told Bonnie that she thought she was crazy. The next week, a social worker took Michelle to Topeka State Hospital for an evaluation. Michelle was scared and did not know what was happening to her life. Katherine went with her to Topeka. Michelle was told that she would stay there for thirty days for an evaluation and be allowed to leave. Michelle made friends with other kids around her age. The kids talked about how they liked messing with the doctor's heads by pretending to be crazy to get medicine. This gave Michelle an idea. Michelle did not want to return to Katherine's home because she could not protect her from Joseph, so she told the therapist who evaluated her that she saw demons in the mirror and heard voices. This was so far from the truth. Michelle just wanted to make sure that she never returned to Katherine's home, she did not know that the therapist would brand her a schizophrenic, put her on heavy doses of thorazine and make arrangements for her to go to Crittendon Children's Home. This was a nightmare. Michelle hated the medication. She was on 1000 milligrams per day, and this made her almost catatonic. Day after day, Michelle would sleep all day, not take care of her personal hygiene, and ate enormous amounts of fattening food. She started to gain lots of weight which she could not loose. Her beautiful hair fell out and would not grow anymore. Michelle turned into a female linebacker. Boys at Crittendon teased her because of her unattractive appearance. Michelle was so out of it from the medication, she forgot what she looked like and was unable to perform simple chores or take care of her personal appearance. Crittendon Home was a place for the rich. Katherine had pulled strings to get Michelle there. She had really good, educated therapists. Her favorite was a lady named Carolyn everyone called Kief. Carolyn saw Joseph for the low life, evil being that he was, and got a court order to have him stop all contact with Michelle. Katherine was the only one permitted to visit Michelle. Michelle was one of three Blacks that were at Crittendon. She felt so uncomfortable there being away from Katherine. Life with white people was different for Michelle. The surroundings at Crittendon were more than comfortable. The holidays were posh, nice gifts were given to every child. They had picnics, Hawaiian Luaus, and each therapist took their group once a month to a restaurant. Michelle had a personal tennis instructor, who took her on trips to the mall and to have her hair styled. Children are often too forgiving and this being the case with Michelle, she had arguments with her therapist about why she couldn't have visits with Joseph. It was like Michelle had amnesia about what had happened to her. She still sought the love of Joseph. Michelle could never really adjust to life at Crittendon and after one year and a half, she asked to leave and go back to Topeka. Once Michelle was transferred, Katherine fought to get Michelle taken off of thorazine. Katherine felt her heart sink seeing her once beautiful, lively daughter turned into a linebacker zombie. All of Michelle's looks had left her, she had the figure of a football player and she had short hair that would not grow anymore. It was like a never ending curse had been placed on Michelle. Therapists at Topeka State Hospital worked with Michelle to get her to face reality about Joseph being a bad influence on her and that they wanted to limit contact of him. Michelle was allowed to attend Topeka High School for two classes a day. She took Math and Choir. Math was never Michelle's strong point, she mostly got D's. Choir was always good because Michelle enjoyed singing. After a few voice lessons, Michelle sang pretty good. There were lots of good looking guys at Topeka High, but none of them ever expressed interest in Michelle. That was a lonely time for Michelle. She watched many dances, but was never invited. Michelle lived at Topeka State Hospital, who would want her? A guy named Donny sort of liked Michelle, but he did not want to consort with her in public because of where she lived. He felt embarrassed to be seen with her. Soon he stopped talking to her altogether when he made the yell-leading team with the cheerleaders. When prom night came, Michelle never went and was never invited. When it was time for Michelle to leave Topeka State Hospital, she went to a posh group home called the villages in Topeka. Joseph was not allowed to visit Michelle there either. Only Katherine and her new husband we to have contact with Michelle. Since Michelle was robbed of a normal life, her self esteem suffered. She had never gone out on a date with a guy her age. No guy in her circle was interested or attracted to her. She never knew how to relate to guys. Up until age 18, Michelle lived in group homes. She did not trust anyone or her reality. Any time things started going good, she'd fear that it would turn evil at any given moment. Michelle graduated from high school with a 3.5 grade average. Shortly after high school, she moved back in with Katherine and attended business school majoring in Business Administration. Joseph would still come around and make life hell for Michelle. He would tell her she was ugly and that no man would ever want her. Death threats were uttered from the evil man's lips often. Katherine was still afraid of Joseph and never confronted him. He had remarried a white woman named Sharon and had four children by her. Death was always near Sharon cause Joseph would snap often and beat the daylights out of her, even when she was pregnant. One day after drinking, Joseph stabbed Sharon with an ice pick in her arms and legs, the poor woman almost died. Sharon often accused him of sexually molesting his daughters, which his mother and family members would deny. Joseph got off into drug dealing and other shady dealings to support himself. Years and years of being in the underworld he became more powerful and untouchable. Even the police and other law enforcement departments turned their heads when it came to Joseph. Rumor had it, that he had protection from the Mafia. If that was true, it was the only thing keeping him alive. A man as dirty and ruthless as him should be imprisoned forever. Michelle moved away from Katherine's and landed a job with a stock transfer agent company. She moved into a posh downtown area and rented a nice loft. She decided to put her troubled past behind her and try to get some happiness out of her life. She did not contact Joseph or his family for five years. Michelle worked everyday and stayed to herself until she discovered an Italian owned nightclub down town. It was only four blocks from her loft downtown. She made it her second home. It was a posh club, with desirable businessmen and dark haired Italian men. This was a dangerous combination for Michelle, it led to her second revelation. Due to the fact that Michelle had no experience with men, for some reason she was attracted to the low-level men of the Mafia and she found one who was the manager of the club she loved called Good Life. Every Friday after work, Michelle would go shopping for a new dress and heels, get her hair done and go to Good Life. She felt glamorous dressing up in that nightclub chasing after the manager. It was lust at first sight when Michelle saw him, he dressed impeccably in dark suits with ties, was very quiet, very good looking and mysterious. Every woman at Good Life wanted to land him, at least be in bed with him. His name was Sal. He was mysterious and untouchable. He wasn't too friendly or accessible; he never took drinks from people, especially strangers. Michelle could tell he was powerful by the way many people showed him respect, by hugging him, saying hello and a few Italian women called him Godfather. For some reason, Michelle became obsessed with Sal. Every waken moment was spent thinking about him. For a long time, Michelle could not get his attention when she was at Good Life. Sal preferred blondes and petite girls. There was always women up under him, a different one every night. Michelle almost gave up on ever meeting him until one Friday night after work. She went to the salon and had her hair done bought a new sexy white dress, white lace stockings and pumps to match. Michelle arrived at Good Life by herself as usual ready to party for the weekend. She met one of the owners of the club, his name was Popeye. He was a tall dark Italian who told interesting stories about him being in the Navy. Popeye was 42, 20 years older than Michelle, she still found him to be attractive. Popeye provided free drinks to her as long as she was in his company. Finally, Michelle got up enough nerve to tell Popeye she found Sal attractive and wanted to meet him. Popeye obliged and Sal and Michelle talked for the very first time. Overwhelmed by his presence, she could not think of a lot of intelligent things to say. Time seemed to fly and before she knew it, she was having a midnight affair with the man of her dreams. Michelle knew exactly what to do to hook him, and it worked. That was not the only night Sal desired to be with her. The relationship was kept low-key for about two years. For awhile, Michelle lost interest in Sal because she a serious lover that did not keep her low-key. Michelle had met her lover through a Columbian drug dealer who was a regular at Good Life. Carlos was his name. He was tall, built like a football player, had dark eyes with black curly hair. He was endowed like a horse and Michelle constantly disturbed her neighbors screaming in ecstasy. This was the best sexual experience in her life. It made her life very enjoyable. Michelle had quit her job at the stock transfer agent company and pursued a career in massage therapy. This turned Carols off and being so, he started to treat her with disrespect. Carlos had a job as a nursing assistant, so he did not make as much money as Michelle did now. Back in the eighties, young masseuses were allowed to work as an apprentice under a licensed professional while they went to school to be licensed. Michelle started working for a well-known shyster by the name of Barb. Barb was ruthless and demanded that her girls work around the clock. Michelle was young and not used to making big money. She had a lot to learn.

The very first night she had five customers and took home $1000.00. She worked for Barb while she took massage classes for about two months. She bought expensive dresses and jewelry and had plenty of money to burn at Good Life. Yes, life was finally good for Michelle. She slept til noon everyday, attended class for two hours then worked after seven in the evening until two in the morning. Her clients were classy businessmen and women who didn't mind spending $200.00 per hour for total pampering. Michelle was classy. She kept her hair and nails beautiful, wore expensive perfume, worked out everyday in her home gym and swam four times a week. She had legs like Tina Turner and was buxom. Michelle was turned off by Black men. They wanted her, but she shunned them. She would not even take Black customers. Maybe Michelle unconsciously did not like her own race anymore due to all of the betrayal she had suffered at the hands of her own family. The second Black man in her life was a Black Hitler. A psycho-beast who she secretly wished the KKK would kidnap and make disappear. At one point Michelle hated Blacks so much, she stopped socializing with all of them. With the exception of one Black guy named Drew, she never dated any Black man. Now she was with Carlos, who didn't want to marry Michelle, he was using her for sex and money. Now that he no longer respected her, he would ask her for a loan every week which he never paid back. Michelle didn't care to much because he acted as her body guard when she opened her own business which she named First Impressions. She ran it with her white girlfriend named Summer. Michelle met Summer through Barb's business. They instantly liked each other and had a lot in common. For none they were both well endowed. This fact kept them out of the corporate world. They were too much of a distraction. Michelle and Summer were too sexy to be in the corporate world working as secretaries. Women would hate them and feel insecure and homely around them and the men would want to bang the hell out of them. So Michelle and Summer decided to work for themselves as masseuses. Since

Summer was white, she always made more money than Michelle, that's just the way it is. In that world if you are Black, to make more money than a white girl, you would need to look like Mariah Carey, Vanessa Williams or Halle Berry. That's just the way of the world in all races, the lighter your skin is, the more attractive you're considered to be. The phrase "the darker the berry, the sweeter the juice" only implies that dark skin Black men have a reputation for being well endowed and being able to bring a woman over the edge in bed. Only Summer would know about this because she dated only Black men for this very reason. For the next few years until 1990, Summer and Michelle ran First Impressions. They lived a posh lifestyle in downtown Kansas City, in a very exclusive neighborhood. Michelle shared a two bedroom condo with Carlos and Summer shared a four bedroom row-house style condo with her lover Jake. They drove expensive cars and took vacations once a month to places like Aspen, Colorado, Scottsdale, Arizona and even Hawaii. Under the table, Michelle and

Summer made $100,000.00 a year. Yes, life was good. One day Michelle visited a massage parlor downtown owned by a very wealthy well known Greek businessman named Gus. Out of curiosity, Michelle asked to talk to someone about employment. A young girl dressed in heels, and a Black satin bikini named Jessie came to greet her in the lobby. She told Michelle to come back to one of the rooms and someone will come to talk to her. About fifteen minutes later, a girl named Cassie came to talk to her. Cassie was eighteen, petite about five food two, 112 pounds with green eyes and light brown hair. Cassie was wearing a white satin thong bikini, with white pumps and gold jewelry. Michelle was curious about the massage parlor and what went on inside. She always heard that the girls who worked at Lite Touch made tons of cash. Rumor also had it that the girls dealt cocaine for high level drug dealers too. Maybe this could explain the brand new Corvettes and Mustangs parked in the parking lot. Michelle told Cassie that she was interested in learning about the massage business. Cassie gave Michelle an application to fill out and a form to take to the health department to be checked for contagious diseases. The owner Gus, came in to introduce himself to Michelle and to tell her to call him for her schedule. Later that evening, Michelle told Carlos that she went to visit Lite Touch massage parlor and he lost even more respect for her and that evening, his price went up. Carlos decided he wanted a Cadillac and asked Michelle for five hundred dollars a week. The next day Michelle visited the health department and passed the exam and called Gus at Lite Touch for her schedule. Gus informed her to start the next weekend. When Michelle returned to Lite Touch to start training, she was a little nervous, not knowing what to expect. No one in that business tells you to your face that when you go behind the doors in those rooms, that you are to let loose the biggest, nastiest freak you have in your soul. Cassie trained Michelle for the first two days. Michelle had to watch her massage men in different positions and doing different techniques, all in the nude. Cassie informed Michelle that you give the customers menu's at the beginning and let them pick the type of massage they want, like an Oriental or Swedish and one was done by getting on a guys back naked and rubbing his body with your knees and inner thighs. You start off in a bikini and pumps, then after you have a customer sign a form stating that he's not paying for sex, get the credit card or cash, you ask him how he would kike for you to dress while you massage him, he usually says "take off the bikini". The massage rooms consists of mirrors on the ceiling and on all of the walls. There are Jacuzzis in all of the rooms, Egyptian cotton white robes, luxurious towels matching the carpet and sheets on the mattress that lies on the floors. All of the powder, oils and lotions are unscented for obvious reasons. Tranquil Oriental or Arabic music plays softly. The rooms smell of lavender oil from the potpourri. A perfect setting to get a man in the mood for a sensuous massage. Michelle learned that mostly the customers wanted to have oral sex with the masseuses and have a hand job and let them have orgasms on their breasts after a rub down in hot oil. These massages were not cheap, they started from twenty minutes up to one hour. The prices ranged from sixty dollars to two-hundred seventy five dollars. Some customers who had unlimited amounts of cash would have two girls massage them. Michelle worked at Lite Touch for awhile until the owner Gus, propositioned her for sex. Michelle was never attracted to Gus and refused his advances and naturally, was fired. So Summer and Michelle had fun running their own massage business in the summer of 1990 until 1992. That's when Michelle went off the deep end with Sal, the manager of Good Life. Every since Carlos got greedy and took two thousand dollars from Michelle's purse, Michelle lost all desire for him and never saw him again. He tried to come back into Michelle's life, but she just didn't feel the same about him. Carlos gave up and went away. Sal and his business associates decided to change the theme on their club Good Life and make it into a gay bar. They named it Club Mecca. This put a damper on Michelle's and Summer's night life for awhile. They didn't like any of the other clubs in Kansas City. It took them a long time to venture into Club Mecca because it was a gay bar. Michelle wanted to go to find Sal. Since she didn't have Carlos anymore, she now hungered for Sal. One Friday night, Michelle dressed up in her black leggings, oversized sweater and black suede pumps and went to Club Mecca to see Sal. He was sitting at the bar with his cousins and told Michelle to come over for a drink. Sal and Michelle made small talk and Sal told her to go downstairs to the first floor bathroom. Michelle did what he said and saw one of her ex co-workers from the stock transfer agent company, named Jackie. She was glad to see her friend. Jackie asked her what she was doing going downstairs, Michelle told her that she left something at Murphy's lounge downstairs. Sal came in the bathroom to see Michelle. He grabbed her and kissed her deeply. Michelle missed him a lot and was glad to be with him. She would settle being this man's mistress until she died, that's how much she loved him. Michelle knew that she could never be with this man in public for one, he was the type of Italian businessman that would be disowned or killed if he wanted or chose a Black wife. Michelle did not know at the time, that Sal was engaged to the grand-daughter of a reputed mob boss. Later that night, Sal picked Michelle up in his BMW and drove her to her condo. They kissed and groped each other, then spent the night together for one last time. From then on, Michelle was no longer allowed in Sal's life. No phone calls were accepted by her and she was not allowed in the club and if she came by, Sal's business owners would come out and threaten her with the police. Devastated, Michelle sat in her loft and did not work as much. She became depressed and started to drink heavily. Michelle could not accept the fact that it was over between her and Sal. She became a pathetic mess. She started calling him at his restraints, he would tell her not to call and hang up on her. She would call fifty times a day at his nite clubs. The staff would call her crazy and hang up on her. One night, it was a cold wintry evening and Michelle was all alone. Summer had moved to Arizona, Carlos was out of her life and Michelle only talked to Katherine once in awhile, because she was so obsessed over Sal. He became her world. Since Michelle wasn't working as much, she took a job as a housekeeper at a posh resort in downtown Kansas City. There at Oasis Resort, she met a Black girl around her age who became a good friend to Michelle. The girls name was Crissy. Crissy was smart and classy. She had one child and lived with her boyfriend. She worked in the mini-bar department. Michelle had to move to a smaller apartment since she paid the rent by herself. It was still in an exclusive area and nice, just wasn't as big. Every Friday, Michelle and Crissy would go to an exclusive area called the Plaza that had posh stores like Nordstom's and Sak's Fifth Avenue. They would go to the Plaza movie theatre to see a show then go to Fred P. Ott's for beer and burgers. Michelle confided in Crissy about how she loved Sal and that he refused to see her anymore. Crissy suggested she find out why and at that, Michelle started sneaking in Sal's new club. This was pathetic, for every time she did this, the bouncer Jimmy would throw her out. So Michelle decided to communicate with Sal by writing letters to him. She would send twenty letters a week along with cards and gifts. Michelle even bought two round trip tickets to San Francisco, California and mailed to him as a gift. Sal never wrote Michelle back except when he had his attorney send her a certified letter asking her to cease all contact with him or suffer further consequences. This did not phase Michelle, she continued to write letters and in one of them stated that no attorney could make her stop. One day in February 1992, Michelle called Sal's secretary at her office and demanded to speak to him. Ms. Hoffmaniz told Michelle to stop calling or the police would come to pick her up. Michelle cursed at the woman and this really pissed Sal off. Sal put on his most expensive Armani suit, got his attorney and went to the district attorneys office where his uncles worked and told them about this Michelle that would not leave him alone. Sal was well known in Kansas City and had clout to back him up. The police departments had respect for him and his family and so did other people involved in the political world. Sal's attorney, Mr. Loya, talked with the district attorney about putting a wire tap on Michelle's phone and bugging her apartment and hired four private detectives to follow her around the clock. Sal was nervous about Michelle and did not know how to handle her. He still cared for her, but had animosity in his heart for her when she found out he was going to massage parlors seeing Michelle's co-workers and not her. When Michelle found this out from Kalua, she was hurt and jealous. Being immature and inexperienced with powerful men, she made a deadly mistake by exposing Sal to his parents and his employees. Michelle was watched day and night and all of her phone calls outgoing and incoming were recorded by Sal and by the police department. She still continued to try to reach Sal by calling twenty times per day. Sal talked to a man he knew and had him sneak into Michelle's apartment to install a camera. He was paranoid and wanted to know who she was dealing with to try to destroy him or was she just a nut. Crissy and Michelle continued to be friends and went out every weekend. Crissy advised Michelle to leave Sal alone before things got out of hand. Michelle also knew a private detective named Kari who did an unauthorized credit check on Sal. When Sal found this out, he wanted to wring Kari and Michelle's neck. Michelle only asked Kari to find out if it was true that Sal had gotten married. One of Michelle's friends informed her that Sal had gotten married to the grand-daughter of a mafia boss. The girls name was AnnaMaria. Rumor has it that the marriage was a business arrangement and that Sal did not love her and that making love to her was unpleasant. The private detective Kari confirmed that Sal married AnnaMaria, this information did not stop Michelle from pursuing Sal. One lonely evening Michelle tried to reach Sal by phone and stated that she hoped his wife dies. This was all on tape. This enraged Sal, but he did nothing to have Michelle killed, which he had the connections to have it done. Sal kept his sting operation quiet, only those who had to be involved knew. His new wife and her family knew nothing about Michelle or where she lived for he knew Michelle would disappear and be killed. Sal cared for Michelle deep down and had to get her professional help. He had to help her let go of him and face that they would never be together again. Michelle would not be welcome in his world and he was not prepared to leave it for her. Michelle had no ideal that her phone lines and apartment was bugged. She was followed around the clock by detectives Sal had hired. Politics were involved, these people wanted to get any kind of dirty laundry past or present on Michelle. Detectives went to her previous residences and schools she attended and interviewed people who knew her. Past landlords were questioned about what type of character she seem to have. Sal had investigators go to the resort where she worked as a housekeeper to interview her co-workers and supervisors. Even her best friend Crissy was interviewed. All of Michelle's personal life was now under a microscope. She worked as a housekeeper during the day and as a masseuse in the evening. She didn't make as much money as she did a few years ago, but it was still a nice living. Luxuries like going out to nice restraints, shopping and vacations were still attainable for her. Everywhere she went, Sal's thugs followed. When Sal's people thought they had enough dirt to have Michelle arrested, they went to her job and told her supervisors they were there to arrest her for questioning. Michelle was terrified and humiliated by the policemen there who handcuffed her in front of customers and her co-worker's.

Jail and prison life was not a lifestyle that Michelle was accustomed to. She was taken to a cell and held until a detective Moss questioned her about her relationship with Sal. Detective Moss asked her why she wrote so many letters to Sal and if she threatened to harm his wife Liza. Michelle could barely answer the questions due to the emotional trauma she was suffering. She had no-one to call to help her. Her uncle who was a criminal judge was warned not to interfere with this case, and was denied access to Michelle when he arrived at the jail. The whole fiasco was a set up to terrify Michelle into leaving town and never contacting Sal again, even if it meant police, detectives and the district attorney had to deny Michelle due process and violate any civil rights she had. Almost all of Michelle's civil rights were violated. After being held in jail for questioning for twelve hours, Michelle was released. One of her mistakes was not leaving Kansas City right then. Instead she acted like nothing happened, and continued to go back to the same job. Strangely, Michelle's popularity increased at her job. Co-workers and even the manager at the hotel would ask her if it was true that her ex-boyfriend was mob connected. Michelle would only reply that she didn't know. Soon Michelle noticed that different people seem to be following her when she went out in public. She considered moving to a nearby suburb called Johnson county. She moved into a nice apartment called Sunnyvalle Village which was near a new hotel she became employed at. Michelle was naïve about Sal's power. She thought moving into Johnson county would make her untouchable to Sal and his dirty policemen. Michelle had a friend inform her that Sal was related by marriage to a mob boss and to be very careful and to disappear. Michelle continued to try to contact Sal by telephone and even talked to his wife Liza. The phone calls were traced and soon Sal sent the police to arrest Michelle at her new job. Again, she was terrified. This time Michelle had to stay in jail for three weeks. It was like a dream, it all seemed so surreal to her. Again, guards would ask her if the man who had her arrested was in the mafia, Michelle did not feel comfortable talking about those matters and always said she did not know. Michelle went to court for the first time and wanted to die. The prosecuting attorney went after Michelle with a vengeance. After five years of no contact, Michelle was advised to contact her father Joseph for help. Nothing had changed after five years, Michelle still did not trust the man. She loathed him as usual. Michelle was too upset to eat in jail and she started to loose weight. One night a jail nurse came in to talk to Michelle in her cell. She told her that the man who had her arrested was involved in the mafia and that's why she was being dealt with the way she was. Michelle decided to call her dad Joseph for help. He was street smart and had a few Italian contacts himself. Joseph came down to see Michelle in jail and told her he would put up her bail which was $200,000.00 for a misdemeanor. This was outrageous. When Michelle got home, Joseph advised her to stay away from Sal or he may have her killed. He also told her that the guards in jail told him that Sal's dirty prosecuting attorney was going to railroad Michelle and have her stay in jail for two years. Michelle still did not runaway as she should have. She stayed around and waited for more punishment. She continued to work her job and go out to eat with friends. Two weeks later, another arrest was made on her job and this time Michelle stayed in the Johnson county jail for three months and was extradited to Kansas City. Michelle was sexually molested by guards at the Johnson County jail. The men would sneak into her cell and drug her, then take turns having sex with her. Then they would take naked photographs of her and post them on the internet. One night Michelle awoke when a guard was opening her cell door trying to sneak in, the guard quickly ran out the door. Michelle was extradited to Kansas City jail and spent three months there. It was just as scary. Michelle went to court with Sal for the last time. No-one was allowed in the court room, only Sal, the prosecuting attorney, Michelle, her public defender and the judge. One night when Michelle was in her cell, she was awakened by the main gate to the module being opened; a man walked over to Michelle's door which was unusual because on the female floors, there are no male guards allowed unless there is some kind of disturbance. This man appeared to be Italian, he looked into Michelle's cell at her. Michelle did not scream. The man went away. Michelle mentioned it to her cell mates and they said that she was crazy. The day finally came when Michelle was set free in October 1993. Kari, her detective friend advised her to move to Boston, Massachusetts. Terrified, Michelle agreed.

Kari helped her purchase a bus ticket and drover her to Greyhound. Michelle was relieved to get on the bus and be miles away from Kansas City, but little did she know, she was being set up and the nightmare was far from over. Michelle was betrayed again. Kari was not her friend. Sal paid Kari to get Michelle to move to Boston because that's where he was moving to in October 1993. Michelle thought she was safe when she arrived at the bus station in Boston. She never imagined in her wildest dreams that Sal had her followed the whole trip and that she would be tortured some more in Boston with him and his dirty policemen. A strange woman approached Michelle at the bus station in Boston and asked her if she needed a place to stay. Desperate and scared, Michelle agreed to go with the lady. The lady took her to her apartment and let her spend the night. The next day the lady told her to go to Andy House, a shelter run by the Catholic church. Andy House was warm and had good staff there. Michelle made friends and got a job at a resort in Boston. Michelle told Kari the detective where she was employed and was betrayed again by her when she informed Sal where she was employed. In a new state on a new job for a week, a man walked into the resort where Michelle was cleaning a room. The man slipped pantyhose over his face and took a knife and closed the front door of the room. Then he went into the bathroom where Michelle was working and demanded she undress and give him oral sex. The man ejaculated into Michelle's mouth then left. Numbness went throughout her body and she felt nauseas. Michelle quickly closed and bolted the front door and called her supervisor to come up. The police came up to the room with the supervisor. A report was taken, Michelle was taken to the hospital and that was the end of the case. Michelle did not even get workers compensation for the emotional trauma. Lawyers were warned not to get involved in the case and try to sue the resort. No one would help her. Michelle was set up by Sal to be attacked. But he still wasn't finished with her. Michelle was clueless to the fact that Sal had followed her to Boston, he had her watched round the clock and followed. Michelle knew that something was wrong, but would have never guessed that this madman was stalking her. She presumed he was happily married to Liza in Kansas City and gone on with his life. Sal was not finished with Michelle. More torture was due her. Michelle found out her phone in her new apartment in Boston had been tapped. A new roommate she had, just disappeared while she was at work. They left a not, but she never heard from them again. It was all so strange. Men would harass her everytime she went in public. People would start fights with her for no reason. For six years, this torture went on in Boston, and Michelle did not move. Michelle got pregnant in January 1998. She went through her pregnancy alone for the most part except for help from co-workers. Daisy, Joseph's mother encouraged her to move back to Kansas City. Michelle started getting harassing letters from Joseph threatening her life if she didn't move back to Kansas City to have her baby. Terrified, Michelle tried to file a police report with the letter as proof. The police were mean to her and blew her off. Joseph was also a madman. He contacted Sal in Boston and told him to get rid of Michelle and steal her baby. Together, Joseph and Sal planned Michelle's funeral. Joseph sent thugs to Boston to stake out Michelle's apartment and to watch her comings and goings. Michelle was nine months pregnant and too tired to really notice any unusual people around her place. Sal kept tabs on Michelle and was waiting for her to have her baby. He hated her and wanted to ruin her life, but first he had to make her suffer. On October 18, 1998, Michelle gave birth to a beautiful baby girl who was mixed with Italian and Black. She named the baby Maryjane. The baby was adorable. She was very light skinned with blue eyes. Michelle loved her very much. When she took the baby home, Sal moved in for the kill. When Michelle went out to the store, Sal had a man go into Michelle's apartment and put PCP and Ecstasy into her milk and juice. The man wore gloves so his fingerprints would not get on anything. He laughed as he walked out the door. When Michelle returned that day and

NEVER ENDING NIGHTMARE 53

drank her milk and juice, "the lights went out". She passed out on the sofa and remembered waking up cursing. The baby slept the whole time. Then the next day, Michelle felt extremely sexually aroused and felt like she needed a lot of sex. She started wandering around outside in her nightgown, totally out of it. She then passed out in the parking lot. Some Mexican gang bangers put her in their car and took her to their rival neighborhood and made her shoot a man with a gun. Michelle was so out of her mind, she did not know what was going on. The men took her back to her apartment complex and into her apartment where her newborn baby was sleeping and took turns having sex with her and had anal sex with her, then left. The people who were watching Michelle let Sal know that she was back in the apartment. Sal ordered another man to go to her apartment and inject PCP into her toe. The man followed his orders and left her door open when he left. Michelle woke up and her baby was gone. She was disheveled, had not bathed in two days, was bloody and was totally out of it. She ran to her doctors office who was next door and asked for her doctor. She was in and out of reality. What she did not know was that Sal, had paid the doctors office to go along with him and convince Michelle that she was crazy and that she never had a baby, that it was all a dream. Furthermore, the doctor convinced her that she needed to be hospitalized for schizophrenia. Michelle signed a paper she believed to be a consent form to be treated for rape, but it was an admission form for the Massachusetts State Hospital. A nurse went to call the paramedics to admit Michelle to the state hospital. They came and took Michelle away and were advised not to take blood tests on her because the truth would be exposed and they would know that Michelle was set up to be ruined forever. Two powerful men who were the real psycho's who had an abundant supply of dirty money along with dirty cops to go along with whatever they wanted. Michelle's baby was stolen by Sal and he kept her and raised her with his new wife who could not conceive. Michelle died from all of the drugs that were injected into her. No one tried to find her relatives, they just buried her in a wooden box in a cemetery for the insane. When Michelle closed her eyes for the last time, Katherine and Henry were there to take their beloved daughter back with them to the place where they lived in peace and harmony with their King of Peace.

ISBN 1-41204600-9

Made in the USA
Lexington, KY
22 June 2011